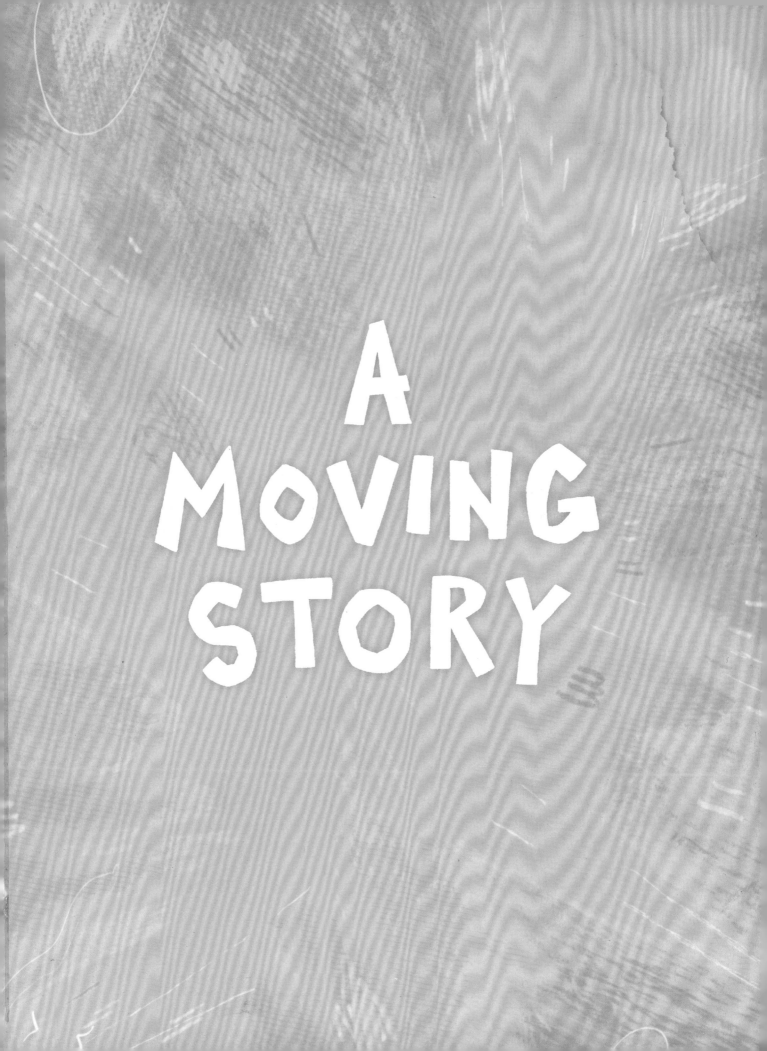

For Amy and Tina, wonderful neighbors, wonderful friends.
—Beth Ferry

To all the crews who take care every day when moving
people from home to home, with special thanks to
those at M.K, who inspired this story.
—Tom Lichtenheld

For Erin, my forever moving buddy.
—Tom Booth

A Moving Story • Text copyright © 2024 by Beth Ferry and Tom
Lichtenheld • Illustrations copyright © 2024 by Tom Booth
All rights reserved. Manufactured in Italy. No part of this book
may be used or reproduced in any manner whatsoever without
written permission except in the case of brief quotations
embodied in critical articles and reviews. For information
address HarperCollins Children's Books, a division of
HarperCollins Publishers, 195 Broadway, New York, NY
10007. www.harpercollinschildrens.com • Library of Congress
Control Number: 2023944779 • ISBN 978-0-06-321866-6
The illustrations were created digitally, using Procreate.
Typography by Chelsea C. Donaldson • 24 25 26 27 28 RTLO
10 9 8 7 6 5 4 3 2 1 • First Edition

A MOVING STORY

gentle GIANT movers

STORY BY

BETH FERRY AND **TOM LICHTENHELD**

PICTURES BY

TOM BOOTH

HARPER
An Imprint of HarperCollins Publishers

PETE AND TINY WERE MOVERS.

Their broad shoulders and strong hands were just the right size for moving things.

Big things.

And tiny things.

Weird things.

Revered things.

Bulky things.

Beloved things.

Anything.

Nothing was too small or too light

to wrap up tight

and treat just right.

The brothers were very well-suited for their jobs.

Tiny had a knack for packing,

an eye for organizing,

and his six-box balancing act never failed to impress.

Pete was a mover who was definitely *not* a shaker.

He had a quiet way that soothed even the most

fretful family.

But both brothers knew there was NO rushing the perfect packing job, which required more *P*s than a packing box could hold:

Padding

Peanuts

Paper

Packaging

Preparation

Protection

Patience

PHEW!

Tiny and Pete were in the middle of one of their biggest jobs ever.

The Panda family was moving.

"Hupsie," said Pete.

"Hoovit," said Tiny.

"Gotter?" asked Pete.

"Gotter!" said Tiny.

"Torky!" said the littlest panda.

Tiny and Pete smiled at the panda and her turtle every time they passed.

And they passed them *a lot* because they were in the groove—

in the groove of a very smooth move.

MOM'S BOOKS

And the only thing that could stop them was some **VERY SMOOTH** . . .

. . .PEANUT BUTTER!

"*Perrrumble*," went Tiny's tummy.

"*Gerrrumble*," went Pete's.

It was lunchtime!

Tiny spread out a blanket while Pete spread the peanut butter.

Then they both spread their arms in invitation.

"Lunchmunch?" Pete asked.

"Yumscrum," the panda answered.

Peanut butter lettuce wraps were her favorite.

Pete showed her how to make firework sounds out of Bubble Wrap while Tiny transformed the packing peanuts into confetti.

The little panda's laughter made it feel like a celebration.

But boxes don't pack themselves, so the brothers packed up the lunch.

And once again they were back in the groove of their very smooth move.

Until something went **WRONG.**

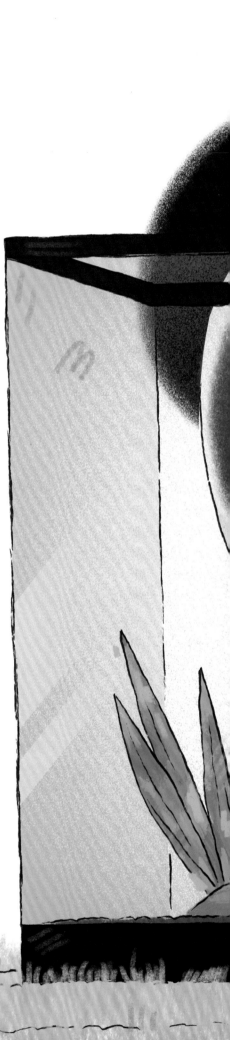

Something went missing!

Tiny had just placed the final box into the truck, fitting it in like the last piece of a puzzle, when the little panda called, "Torky! Wuryoo?"

Her turtle was missing.

"Canoolook?" she asked the brothers, holding up the empty tank.

"Ubetcha," Pete answered.

"Notta frit-fret," Tiny added, patting her head.

"I hep," the little panda said.

The search party searched *everywhere*

until there was only one place left to look.

BOOKS
BAMBOO
BAMBOO
BATH
HANDLE WITH CARE
DINING ROOM
DAD'S OFFICE STUFF
UNDERWEAR
BOOKS
BOOKS ABOUT BAMBOO
MOM'S OFFICE STUFF
BAMBOO
THIS SIDE UP
BEDDING
ATTIC
GADGETS
BOOKS
Tiny

"Torky?" the little panda called. "Indare?"

Tiny stared at his perfectly packed truck.

"Wohnoh," he said, shaking his head.

But Pete was staring at the little panda.

"Tiny . . ." he said softly.

Tiny turned and saw the little panda.

And he remembered that nothing

and *no one*

was too small or too slight

to treat just right.

So the brothers pulled out couches and credenzas

and carton

after carton

after carton.

unrolled rugs,

SOLD

They opened boxes,

and unpacked all their
careful packing.

gentle GIANT movers

But there was no sign of Torky.

And they had no choice but to repack the truck.

"Thank you for trying," Mr. and Mrs. Panda said.

"Hankhoo," the littlest panda sniffed, patting

each brother on the knee.

Pete slowly climbed into the truck.

Tiny followed.

It had been a tough day.

And they were tired.

The brothers were so used to lifting things up
that it felt strange to have let someone down.
Especially a small little someone.

"Dimdoom," Pete said.

"Glumgloom," Tiny agreed.

"*Perrrumble*," went a sound.

Pete looked at Tiny's tummy.

Tiny looked at Pete's.

But it wasn't their tummies.

The sound was coming from the lunchbox.

IT WAS TORKY!

"Woo!" said Tiny.

"Hoo!" said Pete.

They backed up faster

than *zoom-zoom*.

"Dareyago," said Pete.

"Gotter?" asked Tiny.

"Torky!" cheered the panda.

And she wrapped them all in a great big thank-you of a hug.

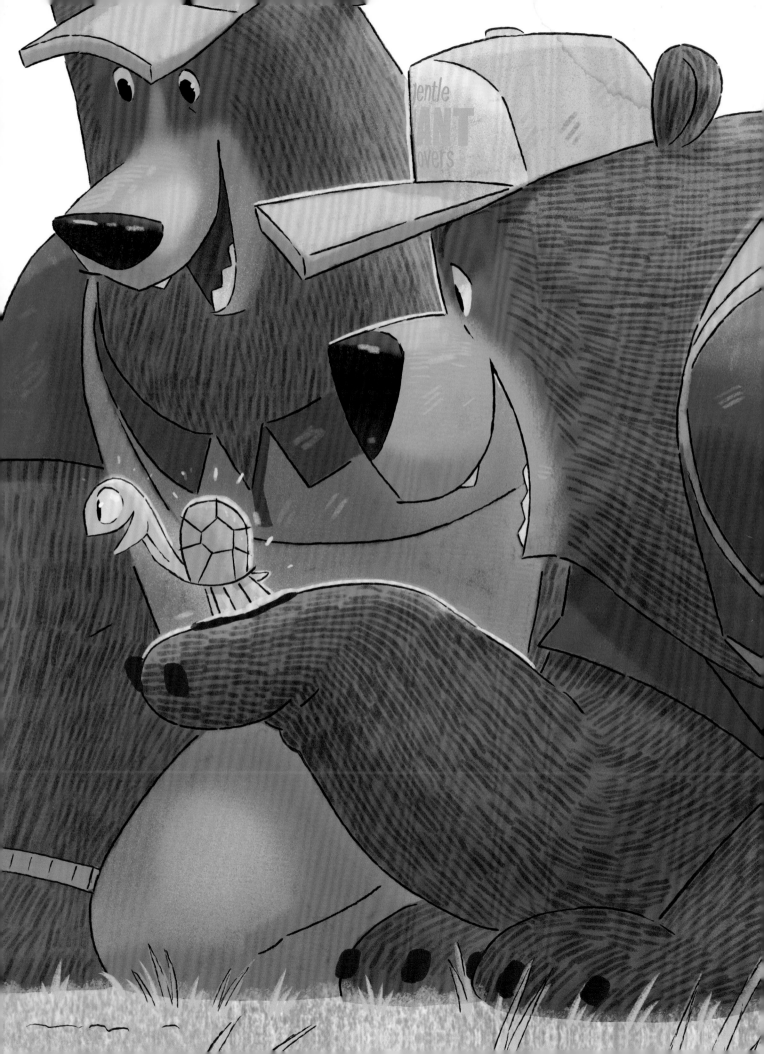

Because nothing and *no one* was too big
to wrap up tight and treat just right.